Pete the Sheep

written by **Jackie French**

illustrated by **Bruce Whatley**

HarperCollins *Children's Books*

First published in Australia by HarperCollins*Publishers* Pty Limited in 2004
First published in paperback in Great Britain by HarperCollins Children's Books in 2007

10 9 8 7 6 5 4 3 2 1
ISBN-13: 978-0-00-722808-9
ISBN-10: 0-00-722808-2

Text copyright © Jackie French 2004
Illustrations copyright © Farmhouse Illustration Company Pty Limited 2004

HarperCollins Children's Books is a division of HarperCollins Publishers Ltd.
The author and illustrator assert the moral right to be identified as the author and illustrator of the work.

Visit our website at: www.harpercollinschildrensbooks.co.uk

Bruce Whatley used watercolour and coloured pencil to create the illustrations for this book.

Printed and bound in Thailand

To Dunmore, a sheep among sheep. JF

To Phoebe, a dog among sheep. BW

Ratso the shearer had
a sheepdog called Brute.

Big Bob the shearer had
a sheepdog called Tiny.

Bungo the shearer had
a sheepdog called Fang.

grrrrrrrr!

But the
new shearer
had a...

'You can't have a sheep-sheep!'
cried Big Bob.

'Why don't you get a
proper sheep*dog*!'
yelled Ratso.

'Strewth!' muttered Bungo,
who never said much.

'Pete's as good as any
   sheepdog,' said Shaun.
'We just do things…
   differently.'

‘baa baa!’ said Pete,

which in sheep talk means,
‘If you don't mind waiting, sir, Shaun will be with you shortly.’

Shaun and Pete were a great team.
Shaun was a sensational shearer,
and the sheep really liked Pete.

'baa baa?' asked Pete.

'Yes, you're right,' said Shaun.
'I do need to take off a little
more around the ears.'

'Well, we do things properly in this shed!'
yelled Ratso. 'Go bring in some sheep, Brute!'

'Hurry up, Tiny!' called Big Bob.

'Yup,' agreed Bungo, who never said much.

But the sheep didn't
move. They were
waiting for Pete.

woof!

arf arff arff!

'That sheep-sheep is nothing but
a troublemaker!' yelled Ratso.

'He has to go!' cried Big Bob.

'Too right!' shouted Bungo,
who never said much.

'If Pete goes, I go!' said Shaun.

grrrr

'That suits us fine!'
yelled the other shearers.

'What will I do now?'
Shaun asked sadly.
'I love shearing!'

'baaaaa!' Pete said comfortingly.
'You're right, Pete,' said Shaun.
'At least I still have you to shear.'

First, Shaun sheared
Pete's front and
back legs.

Then he sheared
Pete's neck and middle.

Then he took off Pete's hat...

...and gave him a whole new look!

When Pete showed it off to all
the other sheep, they were amazed.

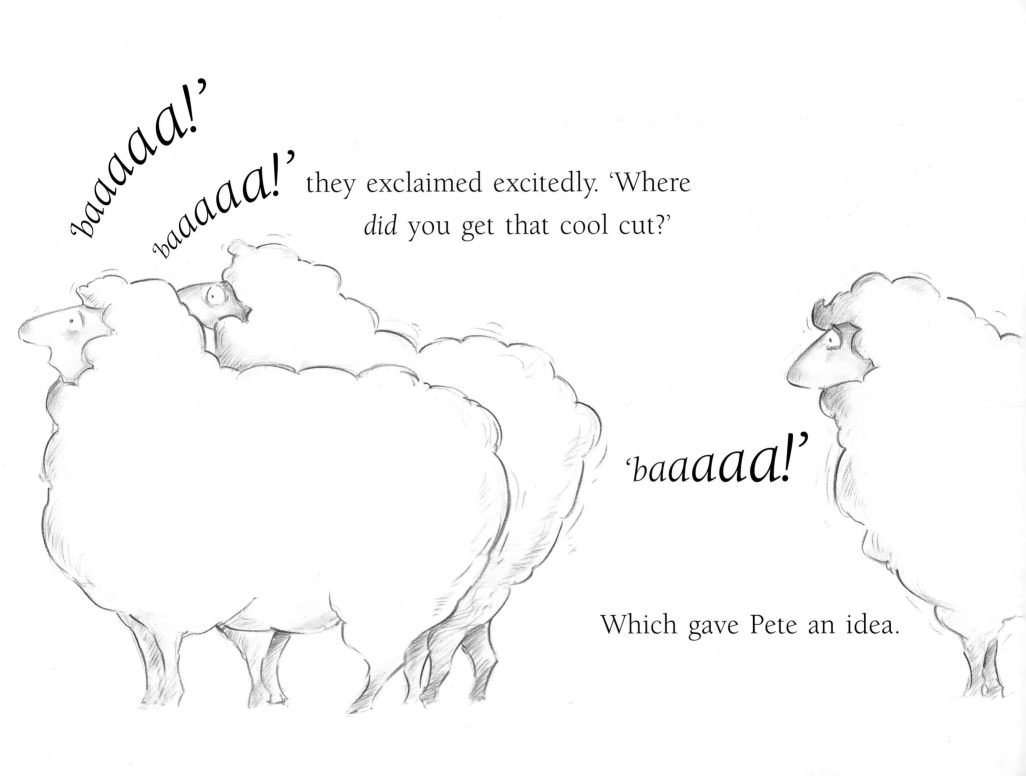

'baaaaa!' 'baaaaa!' they exclaimed excitedly. 'Where *did* you get that cool cut?'

'baaaaa!'

Which gave Pete an idea.

Their first customer
was *very* happy.

So was the second.

And *so* was the third!

Soon, everyone was talking about

Shaun's Sheep Salon.

News of their success spread quickly.
Before long, Shaun and Pete had so
many customers they couldn't look
after them all.

The other shearers were **furious!**

'It's **not** fair!' said Ratso.
'*We're* the ones who have
proper sheepdogs.'

'Too right!!' agreed Big
Bob. He looked around.
'By the way, where
are our dogs?'

'Jumping jumbucks! Look what
I just found!' roared Bungo, which
was more than he usually said in a week.
The shearers raced into town.

The three dogs had crept
sheepishly into the salon.
'woof?' asked Brute hopefully.
'arf,' agreed Tiny.
'grrrr,' added Fang,
admiring a sheep Shaun
had just shorn.
'I'm really sorry,' apologised
Shaun, 'but our salon
is for sheep only.'

'baa baa baaaaa!'

Pete said firmly.

Shaun grinned. 'You're right, Pete,' he said. 'There's no reason why sheepdogs can't look gorgeous, too.'

Shaun had just finished curling Tiny's tail when the three shearers rushed through the door.

'Where's my dog, Brute!' yelled Ratso.

'Where's Tiny!' cried Big Bob.

'Fang!' bellowed Bungo.

'woof!' barked Brute firmly.

'arf arff arfff!' added Tiny.

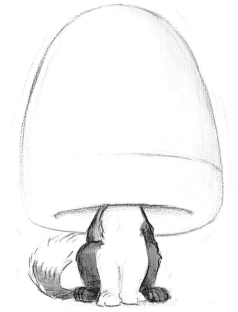

'grrr,' growled Fang, which in dog talk means, 'No way am I leaving till I'm done!'

'What are we going to do?' moaned Big Bob.

'There aren't any sheep left for us to shear,' added Ratso,
'and even our mangy mutts have deserted us!'

'Doggone dogs,' grumbled Bungo.

'baa baaaa!'

said Pete.

In the end, it all worked out happily.

Ratso could shear sheep styles that
were almost as good as Shaun's.
Big Bob specialised in sheepdog styles.
And Bungo learnt how to speak to the clients,
'Oh, madam, you do look lovely!
I only wish everyone could look
as gorgeous as you do!'

'baa baaaa!'

cried Pete the sheep.

He'd had another idea.